SUSPENSE STORIES V2

GREAT SUSPENSE STORIES

ABDUL RAHIM KHURRAM

Contents

CHAPTER ONE

Can we keep him_ Please!

Mark and Marina, Martha's children, were widowed. Mark was in high school and was quite athletic, but Marina was in middle school and was really timid. Martha has been suffering from depression after her divorce from her spouse. She was striving to provide for her children. She's been working on herself and growing better now that she has a new job. She works out, runs, and performs yoga, which makes her feel lot better. She went for a run around the neighbourhood one morning before she had to wake the kids up for school. She glances down at her watch to check the time and accidentally bumps with someone's shoulder.

She apologised to the guy she had assaulted. "Hello?" the guy said as he looked around. "Who did that?!"

"I'm standing right in front of you, sir," Martha adds, concerned.

The guy was about to flee when he felt hands on his shoulder. "WHO'S OUT HERE?!?" he yells in panic.

Martha flees him, all the way to her home. She smashes the front door open, only to be halted by what seems to be a demon. It addressed her in a scratchy voice.

"You don't mean anything to anybody. This is why you are unnoticed. In two hours, I shall inhabit this body and steal the souls of your children."

Tears started to fall down her cheeks, and she cried out for assistance, but no one could hear her.

"Can you hear me, Mark and Marina?" Please respond!" Martha replies, her voice trembling with fear and grief.

As of 8:30 a.m., they're officially tardy for class. Marina awakens at 10:15 a.m. and cannot locate her mother. She starts panicking and wakes up Mark. He is just somewhat concerned till he enters the entrance hallway. He notices blood on the floor and notices that something is constantly touching him. He dials his mother's phone and hears it ring throughout the house. He allows it to go to voicemail and then hears the strangest voice on the recorded line.

"Hello, little child," said an elderly man with a hoarse voice. "Your mother will not be pleased," he laughs. "She'll do it if you do me a favour."

"And what is that?" Mark asks.

"You must bring me your sister's soul," the demon-like voice says.

He can't allow that happen to her, but what would he do if he didn't have his mother?

"Marina doesn't even care about me; when will I ever need her?" he wonders.

Marina approached him, and there was a loud THUMP at the door that rang throughout the house. With a tremendous bang, the door swung open and tumbled to the ground. Martha understood what she had to do at this moment. She was forced to fight. A massive shouting beast of a guy bursts through the door. He is nothing more than a shadow, a monster. Martha attempts to pursue him with a large kitchen knife, but nothing she does stops him.

"I won't let you do it," Mark says as he moves in front of Marina. "You can't have her!"

"I can do everything dumb little guy, I can even bring your mother back," the devil grinned.

His mother appeared beside him. Mark attempted to assist her. The devil comes above her and possesses her with his first stride. Martha comes up to Mark and Marina and warmly embraces them.

"You're not our mother," Marina says as she takes a step back.

"No, I'm not," Martha responds, "but I have your mother's brain in my mind, and she wouldn't do anything to protect you anyhow."

She was gone in the blink of an eye. Mark shouts at Marina to come with him. They dash out to his vehicle, and he drives for many hours. They end up at a Montana motel. Only a few states away from their Nevada home. They used their mother's credit card to check in and travelled down numerous corridors to locate their room. The moulded pores in the ceilings were leaking with what seemed to be unclean water. The lingering odour of cigarette smoke, with nicotine yellow walls.

"Well, it makes sense that the bill for the night is just fifty dollars," Marina adds. They cast a disdainful glance about.

Mark is the first to enter the room and moves up to the nightstand in between the beds. He tries to switch on the light, but it merely flickers. Marina flips on the light switch. Mark yells in surprise. The devil arrives and sits on the bed.

"What do you want with us!!" screams Mark.

"I merely want your soul," the devil snickers. "Is that too much to ask?" he asks, smiling sinfully.

"Where is our mother?" Marina interjects.

"Don't listen to him!" says Martha, echoing around the room. "Save yourself." Mark and Marina are perplexed as they glance around.

Marina shouts, "Mom, where are you?!?"

The guy at the front desk notices a lot of noise. He walks inside their room and knocks, saying, "Is everything all right in there?"

The monster throws Mark against the wall across the room as he is about to shout back. When the guy goes in, he notices Mark resting on the floor. He starts to speak something but is cut short, blood seeps to the floor, and the guy dies. The devil is behind him, blood on his palm, and he lets out a yelp. Mark notices that the devil has torn the man's heart out.

"No one will ever be able to assist you. Don't you notice? Simply give me what I want, and you will be set free." According to the devil.

Marina, who is assisting Mark, then asks, "And what do you want?"

"I want a soul; I've already taken your moms and need one more to complete..." "The procedure," the demon stammered.

Mark hears his mother say softly, "I know what you have to do to stop him." Go to the cemetery at precisely 12:01 a.m. You and Marina must then say, "I want you to reveal yourself, in the name of the Holy Spirit, SHOW YOURSELF!" to the devil that is inhabiting this family.

To gain time, Mark adds, "Fine, we'll locate you a soul." Please give us 24 hours." The Demon then vanished.

"What was the point of that?" "We cannot give that horrible creature someone's soul!" Marina moans.

In order to avoid risking her life, Mark tells Marina, "Don't worry about it I'll take care of it"

"I want to know what you're thinking!" Marina insists. "How are we going to proceed?"

Mark pretends to sleep, so maybe she'll give up and fall asleep. She is correct. He wakes up at 11:00 p.m. and walks to the nearby graveyard. Marina, he has no idea, is not sleeping. She had been discreetly following him in the shadows.

When he reaches the middle of the cemetery, she asks, "Mark, what are you doing out here?" He finally caved and told her what Martha had said. Marina became enraged and said, "Why wouldn't you tell me?" before adding, "We're meant to be in this together!" It's our mama! You must give me this information so that I may assist you!"

As Mark confesses with great sincerity, "I WAS JUST TRYING TO PROTECT YOU."

"Both of you listen!" Martha arrives out of nowhere. You must do this task IMMEDIATELY!"

The time has passed and it is now 11:59 p.m. "To the devil inhabiting this family, I ask you to present yourself, in the name of the Holy Spirit, show yourself!" Mark and Marina hold hands and begin chanting.

And then the devil emerges for the first time. They repeat it again and over. The devil is shrinking and seems to be terrified. "You idiot youngsters don't know what you're doing!" he laughs uncomfortably.

Mark and Marina are deafeningly deafeningly deafeningly deafeningly deafeningly deafeningly deafeningly deafeningly They come to a halt as the monster becomes inferior, and Martha creeps up behind them. They exchange hugs. Martha then takes a mason jar from her bag. She approaches the little little evil thing and places him in the jar.

"Can we keep him?" Mark inquires.

"No, we're going to bury him somcwhere no one can find him," Martha laughs.

They bring him home, go to their local cemetery, dig a deep hole in the middle, and bury him. Martha, Marina, and Mark return home to clean up the shambles. Finally, they all fall asleep.

Martha gets up the following morning eager to go for a morning run. As she runs, she accidently runs into a man, and she becomes concerned since he won't be able to see her. When he notices her, he says, "Hey," in a flirtatious tone, and adds, "Would you want to run with me and maybe have some coffee afterwards?"

"I'd love to," she says, accepting.

CHAPTER TWO

Deadly gift

When I opened the front door, the real danger began. The six-six monster has been haunting my fiancée for more than a year beneath my porch. His nose was drenched with raindrops while the hairs of his buzz cut stood on edge. I could see by the look on his face that opening the door had been a mistake by the way he had his jacket collar pulled up.

When I attempted to come up with a way to defend myself or warn him away, nothing came to me. First to speak, he.

'It's a nice evening, isn't it, Dan?'

Looking over his shoulder, I saw a thick layer of rain sticking to the obsidian roof tiles of the buildings across the street.

'Eh..'

He grabbed my chest with his frying pan-sized palm and forced me back into the hallway of my own home.

'Dan, are you here?'

As he pushed me against the wall, closed the door behind him, and turned the key in the lock, I shook my head and sighed in frustration.

What about just the two of us?' That's not so horrible, after all.'

What do you think?‘ he said to Tom.

’Think carefully,‘ he said. ’I’ve already told you that.‘

There was a brief hush. He walked into my living room, removing his hand from my chest. While sitting on the sofa, his boots were propped up on the table.

’Are you not going to do anything kind for your old friend?‘

After what seemed like an eternity of staring, I finally realised what he had said.

If you’d want tea with that, Tom?

Just two sugars and no milk this time, please.

I nodded, turned on my heels, and prepared a cup of tea for the guy who had made my life a living hell since Chloe and I were romantically involved. When I returned to the living room, he had the longest knife I’ve ever seen between his knees. When I realised how he got it into my house, I worried how I might get out of this predicament.

Throwing tea in his face, I grabbed the table lamp next to me and smashed him over the head with it till the plug sprang from the wall and wrapped around my waist. Tom’s bloodied cranium flopped to one side as he lay on the ground, his black jacket shoulder dripping with it. Although Tom had been eliminated, this was hardly a moment to celebrate.

The light was tossed away from me once I unwound the cable from my body.

’Oh fuck, oh sh*t, oh holy sh*t,‘ I thought.

I sat on the armrest of the chair next to the bleeding mess of a guy I’d dreaded for so long, staring at the gruesome scene. The only thing that occurred to me was how much smaller he had become. I had no doubt I’d have to get rid of the corpse. I had no intention of reporting this to the authorities. Because they don’t get it, they may cause

Chloe to have another miscarriage. No, the police did not need to know about this.

Because digging a grave alone would take too long, I realised I couldn't do it. I needed to speak with someone who could empathise with me and whom I could rely on. In my pants pocket, I pulled out a phone and started scrolling through the contacts on the screen. Lee. The husband of Chloe's mother, who was in Barcelona with her for a girls' weekend.

I had the foresight not to call him from my cell phone. Those records would reveal that. Because of a planned bicycle ride to Kerry, I had purchased a vintage Motorola flip-phone. I'd never heard of it before.

The bottom drawer of my bedroom locker was open as I dashed up the stairs of our modest dormer house. To my surprise, I was able to grab the white cardboard box after dumping my underpants on the floor. In the rear pocket of my sweatpant-clad pants, I shoved my phone and charger.

There was a long, grimy swath of blood at the bottom of the stairwell. To my right, I saw a living room. Tom, not at all. Chloe had insisted that we preserve the phone stand, so I swivelled my car around and followed the trail to it. We'd never gotten around to getting rid of our landline, either. Tom grabbed for the phone with one hand while standing at the foot of the stand.

I sprang off the steps and placed my foot on his back, causing him to fall backwards. Moaned, he I was nearly moved to compassion for him. In order to further damage his skull, I swung the landline from the wooden stand over my head and repeatedly smacked him in the back of the cranium. My black and white tiles looked like the floor of the world's most expensive slaughterhouse by the time I was done.

To my surprise, he didn't have any money in his pockets. An iPhone, some cash in a wallet. Fires I had just started seconds earlier were all that was left of them when the man knocked on my door. When I saw Tom's face, I was tempted to put him in the grate as well, but I knew that the stench of burning flesh would not be mistaken. This is a foregone conclusion.

Sitting in an armchair in the living room, I took a moment to relax. Flipping the Motorola open, I plugged in my own phone and sat back. I dialled Lee's number as soon as the phone came to life, which took longer than I recalled.

He finally picked up after four rings. 'Hello?'

'Lee. The name of this person is Dan.'

Is there something wrong with you?' a concerned Dan asks. 'Is everything okay with you?'

'So, what do you think?'

'Why don't you call from your own number?' I said. Thanks to my quick response, you have your answer.'

'I need you to come over,' he said, urging him. 'Then, I'll explain.'

He chuckled as he said, 'Come on over,' and I complied. Is it eleven already?' 'Thanks for awaking me,' I said.

I'd underestimated the passage of time.

Listen up, this is critical. 'I need you here.'

When I see you, I'm beginning to get a little tense.

In order to be a true friend, you must assist me out this one.'

He muttered, 'Jesus.' 'How am I going to handle Sarah?'

What? An au pair?' I asked. There are several things that Sarah can do for the baby if she wakes up.'

After a moment of stillness, I could hear him sigh.

The only reason I'm coming is because you're Sarah's godfather. Okay, I'll come over.

Thanks,' I said. 'See you later.'

He answered, 'Yeah,' and then hung up.

Turning the phone over and slamming it on a coffee table, I flung away what was left of it in the ashes of a blazing fireplace. It sounded like my favourite cereal when it popped and crunched.

Prior to Lee's arrival, I mopped the hallway and the living room with bleach. This will have to wait until later, after gazing at the blood-stained sofa in my living room for fifteen minutes. Lee would be appalled by the mess I'd caused, so I decided to cover up the corpse with a sheet. As luck would have it, I happened to have exactly the proper amount of fabric to cover a person. The hammer and the saw were underneath it in our hardware closet. "Who knew?"

Lee appeared at my home 45 minutes after I phoned him. After attaching the two pieces of tarLeein, I heard a knock.

'Dan,' he whispered loudly through the letterbox. Let me in, please.'

I dusted my clean hands on my slacks and slid the door open as I got up.

So I grabbed his arm and yanked him in. Afterward, I locked the door and pushed it shut.

'Fuck. I can smell bleach and raw flesh in here.'

I glanced at him. 'Lee, you're not too far off the mark.'

Now that you've explained it, what's going on?

'Wait a sec,' I replied and pushed by him into the kitchen. In the kitchen, I dragged the corpse across the floor and slammed the legs against the doorway.

It was then that I realised what was going on and took a step back into the hall.

He gazed at the corpse, then turned back to look at me, his eyebrows low, creating shade. 'Fuck. 'Is it a corpse there?'

In other words, "Alright?" The reason he's dead is a good one.'

'For a good reason? In a panic, someone is found dead.

'You're telling me.'

Again, he swivelled his head around to gaze at the corpse, as if to confirm its presence.

'Who . . . who is it?'

Sitting there on the phone stand I used to kill Tom, which was in surprising decent condition, I thought about what I wanted to say.

That Chloe's ex-boyfriend who stalked her and intimidated me?' he reminisces.

As he lay on his back on the stairwell landing, he nodded.

When he arrived at my door last night with a knife the length of my arm, I was terrified.' As soon as Chloe arrived home he threatened to murder me and then Chloe.'

'Fuck.'

'Yes, I am aware. Anyway, the name of this cretin was Tom-'

'I remember.'

'Well, the bastard left me no choice, you know? 'Really, it's self-defense.'

The cops have been called? he inquired, running his fingers through his hair.

Then I responded, "I can't," and shook my head. 'The stress of it may trigger another miscarriage for Becks.'

'Jesus, you're the best.' 'Do you understand what you're saying?'

I sighed and stared at my beautifully cleansed hands. They may be considered as almost too clean.

I said, 'Yeah.' The truth is, I know what I'm talking about. To aid with the ah... burial, so to speak, I've brought you in.'

'Listen,' Lee replied, rising up. Thank you for all of your support throughout the years. During Eleanor's cancer treatment last year, this was great, but I'm not going through with it now. Involved in the killing of someone? That's not going to happen. It's time for me to go. And I'll be going to the cops.'

I tripped him up as he made his way to the door.

As soon as I said it, she looked at me like I was crazy. 'And you're going nowhere. To add to the fun, a little misadventure may be amusing.'

As I stood over him, he pulled himself to his feet. He cocked his fist in my direction and turned to face me. Using my belt, I pulled out Tom's knife. I looked him down.

'Not a great way to treat your closest buddy, is it Lee? 'It's not a pleasant experience.'

'What's the problem?'

Keep your large lips closed and let's get this over with. There is no time to waste.'

Think you're going to be able to scare me?

I jerked my head back and yelled, "You don't help dig that grave." Now I shall put an end to your existence. 'My godchild will be without a biological father.'

My heart goes out to you. I don't know what happened to you. Because of it, you've changed a lot since then.'

No way, Jose. I raised the knife and yelled, 'Don't you fucking dare.'

'Alright, alright,' he said, raising his hands to his face as if trying to hide his disappointment. 'I'll be there.'

Having lowered the knife once again, I proceeded to cut. This is a step in the right direction.

'However, I am only a pawn in this saga, and I want to leave as soon as I can.'

I nodded, placing the knife back from where it came.

'And listen, I won't go to the police. After all,' he replied, rising up, 'what are friends for?'

For the new shed I was constructing in my backyard, I grabbed a spade I had just purchased. Isn't it amazing how things work out from time to time? I placed the tool on top of the corpse and then Lee and I hauled the body outdoors.

'What the hell,' he murmured as we neared the bottom of my garden. 'You have the grave dug already?'

'No, no,' I said. 'These are the foundations for the new shed. "The concrete will be placed tomorrow.""

Glancing at the bags of concrete that lined the pit's outer perimeter, he said, 'Hmm.

We gently lowered the body into the open hole after tilting it so the spade landed on the grass. For a long time, we knelt there, staring into the eyes of death.

'Now,' Lee replied, righting himself. The best thing for me to do right now is to get out of here.

Fumbling for the spade in the dark I whispered, "Okay." 'Thank you, thank you, thank you!'

In contrast, Lee stayed firmly planted on the ground as I rose to my feet. The white of his eyes traced the outline of the garden spade in my hands as he slowly wrung his hands on his jacket.

'By the way,' he said. 'What's the spade for?'

Lee's head was snapped back and he fell into the pit with a wet thud as a result of the spade slipping out of my hands in that split second. He didn't move when I gazed over the edge. My next step was to get down on my hands and knees, cut open three bags of concrete, and cover the two men I knew to be the biological fathers of my unborn child. I couldn't figure out which of them had committed the crime against Becks. This way, I didn't have to worry myself to death.

I finished up the concrete with the spade's flat edge. Even if it wasn't ideal, it would have to do for the time being. I was utterly tired after the night's antics, so I walked back inside, shut the door, and slept until nine the next morning. I ended up destroying the sofa Tom died on, legally discarding it, and getting a new one before Chloe got back from her vacation two days later. When she finally returned, she appeared to be in a state of euphoria.

When Chloe returned home, Eleanor was there to greet her. He's been silent for a few days now and she inquired about him, which made me laugh, because I hadn't heard from him either. A few minutes later, she left without having a cup of tea. Becks informed me that the baby had kicked during the flight home, and she was overjoyed that I had completed the foundations for the new shed in time.

On that particular day, as we sipped our tea outside in the garden, we marvelled at the prospect of our future happiness. Together, we realised an important milestone had been reached, and we were eager to embrace the future. While sipping my tea, my mind wandered to the pit where I had buried my only friend. As I dumped the remaining brown liquid on the freshly laid cement, I nearly wept with sadness over our friendship's demise. But you know what they say, one door shuts, another opens.

Days, weeks, and months passed without anything extraordinary occurring in our lives. Each of us was interrogated about his disappearance after Eleanor made a missing persons report with the police. No one seemed to think much of me, and the police quickly moved on to questioning my other close friends and acquaintances.

It was the first birthday of my baby daughter – and she is my girl because I raised her - when my door was virtually wrenched from its hinges.

Open your mouth, Mr. Reilly. I am an officer with the Garda Sochána (National Police Service).

Our daughter was staring in awe at her first birthday cake when I looked up from the video I was taking of her. Her stunned expression will stay etched in my mind forever as I patted her on the head and winked at her.

Let it go, I told her calmly. The most likely explanation is that you're trying to learn more about Lee.

I slammed the door wide open. 'Yes?'

My hands were told to be outstretched by a hulking police officer. I inquired what it was about.

'I am detaining you in connection with the disappearance and alleged murder of Lee Shank . . .'

My elderly neighbor, Mrs. Jefferson, was suspicious of my "rash and often distrustful behavior of late" because of the construction of my garden shed over a year earlier and its connection to the disappearance of my best friend. What are the chances?

Because my new cellmate is making too much noise, I can't finish this fairy tale of true love with a happy ending and tell you all about my lengthy trial at this time. I believe he should be asked politely to stop talking, so that's what I'm going to do. I had a great time chatting with you.

CHAPTER THREE

Death's Angel

It had taken all year, but now it was finally here. As I lowered the blade to my thigh, a grin pulled at my lips. Picking up my eyeliner, I applied it to my eyes as I reflected in the mirror. My face lights up as I relax my shoulders. Perfect. Standing back from the mirror, I straightened my corset and turned to check out my sleek black pants, which looked amazing. My wings, which are black as darkness, glimmer in the light of my gaze. The door to the restroom swings open, and I turn to see footsteps behind me. Eyes that are as clear as the ocean and a grin as wicked as vice fill the room. His arms are crossed as he leans against the doorframe and opens the door fully. I mimic his posture and grin as I lean on the counter.

All right?

I raise my brows in a stern expression. This being your busiest night of the year, I feel obliged to inquire.

He shrugs, causing his shirt to sag as a result of the motion. I'm drawn to it. His chest beckons to my hungry gaze. He's perfect, you guys.

This has been a part of my life for a long time now. It's no longer a source of anxiety for me. It's your second time, however."

I step in front of him and place a palm on his chest while I do what he instructs, shrugging my shoulders in agreement.

It's safe to say that I was taught by the finest. When he looks at me, I lift mine to meet his. In other words, "I have nothing to fear."

Then he uncrosses his arms and reaches out, putting his arms around my waist and bringing me closer to him until I'm completely engulfed in him. He smiles. It's like I'm flapping my wings and then putting them back in place. Before returning his look to me, his eyes catch sight of the movement and glitter.

As for your talents, I'm not concerned at all. "The rest of it worries me."

Laughing, I snort as I put my arms around his neck. My emotional and psychological health is something you'll have to check in on later tonight, I'm afraid."

Yes, it is.

I lean in close till my lips are only inches away from his, but he's too tall. As the Grim Reaper, I'm saying, "That is what I'm saying."

In order to get a sweet kiss from him, I put my head back and allow him to drop his head to mine.

"Be wise, my darling," your mother said.

As I pass by him to the front door, I let out a sigh. I turn around, my hand still on the knob.

'I've always been there for you, my darling,' she said.

My body is pounding to the rhythm of the party's music. I take a quick look around the room. People crawl and slither against one another in every direction. The smothering shroud of sex and anxiety hangs heavily in the air. I can tell someone is watching me. Turning my head, I see what's on the other side. My gaze meets the bloodshot eyes of a pale-looking guy. I mentally grumble as he makes his way across the floor to where I stand. My wings are tucked in and I have a cup in my hand as I recline back against the wall. I give him a side-glance as he rides up to my side.

At a party like this, what is a lady like you doing with yourself?

When he talks, his tone is slurred. I snort and shrug. When I heard that vampires could drink, I was shocked.

His eyes light up, and he leans against the wall next to me.

"You're one of them," he tells her.

As I continue to search the room, I don't say anything. "You're not going to cause a fuss, are you?" he said

I see his hands in his pockets as he moves and I turn over to see him.

Turning around, I lean against the wall with my knife concealed from his view, arching my brow.

To which he responds, "You know what? If you do, I'll shoot you." As he reacts, I observe. He has a youthful appearance, but he also has a youthful outlook on life.

"It's just been a few months since your last visit."

Turning, he grimaces and sighs.

It was only a week ago that this happened." "He finally acknowledges it, if grudgingly. "Then, out of nowhere, a girl appeared. "The next thing I knew, I woke up in a different state."

I pay attention to his body language and facial expressions. I nod my head in agreement. Inquiry: "Have you signed up yet?"

He raises his brow at me.

"Who did you register with?"

Before responding, I take a sip from my cup. "The Undead Ministry."

In an effort to keep the laughter from spilling out, he twists his lips and puckers his mouth. As he eventually comes to a halt, I inadvertently look away.

What are you talking about? Harry Potter would have been very at home in that scene!

Before returning to him, I place my cup on the table next to me.

So many of us live together peacefully, don't you think? Then then, do you really want to be surrounded by inebriated college students and scary elderly guys at this party? No. The purpose of my visit is to do a task."

As my words begin to sink in, his eyes widen.

I let out a sigh and stroke him on the shoulder.

Come to Café Debinior tomorrow afternoon and I'll show you how it's done. "

My senses begin to tingle as soon as I see a person enter the room. Because he turns toward the figure as I take a step away, the man must have felt it. Before I'm completely out of his sight, I give him a last look.

To which he responds, "Try to avoid biting anybody tonight," with a grin. Then I vanish into the throng, following the figure's trail behind me in the crowd.

Keeping the person in my line of sight but far enough back that it can't be seen, I walk slowly. I use the screaming music and strobing lights to my advantage, blending in with the shadows. When a person enters a room, I pause. Once I've made sure no one is following him, I traverse the distance and quietly enter the room.

Using my wings to make myself utterly undetectable in the dark, I lean against the door. His shoulders slump and his stance droops as he moves to the desk in the room.

A huge sigh can be heard coming from his mouth. The desk light is turned on, illuminating him with a lovely glow. I keep an eye on him. When he looks at the lines criss-crossing his face, his eyes are drawn to them. He uses the soles of his palms to massage his eyes. He gasps as he removes them from his grasp.

It is with a grin on my face that I tear myself out of the cocoon of darkness. He reclines farther back in his chair, separating himself from me. Honestly, it's a pity. He has no choice but to stay. My hair falls forward to frame my face as I go forward and lay my hands on the tabletop. I raise an eyebrow at him.

Is there anybody you're expecting?

He sighs, but he doesn't pick up the phone that's sitting on the desk and call out.

As I see his response, I cock my head. Inquiringly, "Why aren't you terrified of me?"

He laughs. His pupils flicker.

"Because I know exactly why you've come here."

My brows furrow in wonder. That didn't occur to me. "Really? Please explain me what I'm doing here, then.

I can feel his eyes following every curve and crease of my body, finally coming to rest on my chest.

"You want a better grade in my class," the teacher said.

He chuckles quietly, as if he saw something in my eyes.

"Don't be alarmed. It's not the first time. Thank goodness I'm in a giving mood tonight.

I take a step back from the desk as I see he is staring at me. A student once asked, "Is it customary for a professor to hold parties and encourage minors to use alcohol?"

I turn around in my chair and he shrugs as he sits there.

The question is, "Is there a better way to connect?"

I sit on the desk's cdge with my arms crossed. In other words, "Or you'll be subjected to blackmail."

In response to what I've stated, his brow furrows in thinking. He seems to be reconsidering his position. When he sees the dagger fastened to my thigh, his eyes widen.

"What's your name?"

I snort a little. "At first, I believed you were a female attempting to go ahead in class."

His gaze is drawn to mine.

"Don't try to trick me. "What are you looking for?"

As I scan the dimly lit room, I twist a strand of hair with my finger. What you did was wrong, and you should be ashamed of yourself. As I return my sight to him, I soften my voice. "I'm here to get it back for you."

His body stiffens, but his eyes remain still.

As far as I'm concerned, I don't get what you're saying."

As I go closer to him, I put my hand on the desk.

"Isn't it?" I'm well aware of your nighttime activities... You're not being very professorial, are you? Return it, and I may be able to help the others forget about the sins you have perpetrated."

I push him back into the chair with one hand on his shoulder and one foot on his thigh as he jerks to rise.

I tsk as I place my lips on his ear and lean in. There will be no such thing as a discourse like that in this case. "How can I find it?"

"Why would I want to tell you? With me, you'll feel more secure. "I'm on board with it."

I squint my eyes and draw away. In my opinion, that is not what I'm looking for.

Before he can react, I've stabbed him in the back of the neck with my dagger. My attention is drawn to the medallion on his neck, which was covered under his shirt.

In spite of his efforts, I maintain my composure.

I'm not sure what to make of this.

I grab the medallion from his chest and remove it away from him. He reacts with a jerking of his body.

Let me get this straight—"

While removing his neck chain and holding the medallion in the lamp's light, I correct him by saying "Angel.

As I remove the pendant from my pocket, I can feel his angst rising. I look back at him, and I can see that terror has taken hold of me. Nothing can be done to shield him from this.

How will we handle you now?"

He clenches his jaw, but he doesn't respond to the question.

"Hmm. We're not that chatty anymore, are we?"

In one swift motion, I cut through his heart and lungs with my knife. He trembles in his seat. When he closes his eyes, I can hear the tense swallows in his throat.

"I'm sure you know." Softly, I express what I mean.

His eyes widen in surprise as he realises what's happening. He gives a little nod.

"You are aware that death is inevitable...

despite the fact that you've attempted to get away with it. You've done a slew of felonies in the process. In order to survive, how many people have you harmed?"

No response, but his skin warms up and eyes harden as he stares at her in silence.

I chuckle and raise a smirk.

"You don't feel like revealing your secret?" That's OK. Once you're dead, you may come out and admit your guilt."

As I lift my dagger, he snorts.

Are you so certain in your ability to murder me? As far as I'm concerned, you're just another chick."

I take a moment to reflect.

“No. "I am the devil's messenger."

With that, I stab him in the neck with my blade, sending a splatter of his blood over my flesh. It spreads throughout the whole room. I get up from the desk and walk away, whirling my hand to reposition myself. As I move my fingers over the blood patterns, I see the fatal cut I gave him transform into a burrowed furrow over his neck as I adjust my arrangement. Then, when I'm pleased, I conjure up a handgun that appears in his hand. I take a step back and admire my efforts. Suicide should be implied by this.

My hand reaches into my pocket and I gaze down at the medallion.

Wasn't it obvious to you that we were going to capture you?

Put it aside, and I notice it vibrating. As I leave the workplace and return to the party, I smile broadly. My favourite holiday has always been Halloween.

CHAPTER FOUR

Desires

Her heart started to beat faster, and her palms began to perspire. The universe seemed to contract under her feet and over her head. She hurriedly turned and dashed home to avoid shame. She flung open the front door, dashed inside, raced up to her room, and slammed her bedroom door shut, shaking the whole house. As she sat to read a book, she heard light footsteps ascending the stairs, each step creaking and dust flying out into the open. There was a soft knock and the door slowly opened.

"Billy," her mother said softly, "are you all right?" What is the matter?"

Billy shook her head regretfully and lowered her eyes to her tear-stained book as the words started to smear. Her mouth released a little voice.

"I'm good," she said, lowering her gaze to the book. The mother gave a tiny grin, quietly locked her door, and returned downstairs. She climbed into her bed and tucked herself behind her pink cover. She then heard a shout bounce off the walls and echo up into her room minutes later. "Come downstairs for supper, Honey," her mother said.

She collapsed off her bed and slid on her blue and white slippers. She rushed down the stairs and into the kitchen, where a well set table for three awaited her. As she slid over the tile floor, her slippers made a faint tapping sound. She greeted her father graciously after a hard, stressful day at work. As they do every other night, they all sat down.

"How was your day, Dad?" billy inquired.

"I'm OK," he said, sadly. "How was yours?"

"Mine was fine, too," Billy said, cautiously attempting not to dampen the atmosphere any more.

billy knew something was amiss with her mother as the talk progressed. After a lengthy period of denial, she decided to inquire as to what was upsetting her. She responded by stating that she had a very busy day. Billy was aware that something else was hurting her, but she chose not to dwell on it.

Later that night, when she crept down the dark corridor to bid her parents good night, she was stopped dead in her tracks. She picked up on murmurs emanating from their chamber. billy could make out just a few words of their exchange, but she could tell by their tone that they were both unhappy. After a time of listening, she realised they were speaking about her.

"We cannot remain here since she is bullied practically daily. We cannot continue to treat her this way," her mother said angrily. Billy felt really bad as a result of this. She felt utterly powerless. They were relocating as a result of her. This was all her fault. With her head down, she marched back into her room.

billy considered how unjust this was. How she deserved none of this. She hoped she could just open her voice and demand an end to her bullying. To just abandon her. However, she was scared. They would never come to an end. And she was unable to intervene.

At times, she wished she could just vanish. Simply begin again. She stared out into the dark sky that night, as the rain hammered on the glass. She had an idea when a shooting star darted across the darkening sky.

"I desire to be invisible," she said to herself. She prayed this would come true as her mascara spilled down her cheeks. Perhaps, just perhaps, she might abandon her existence. She may just vanish. As her feet landed on the chilly wood floor, she strolled casually over to a painting nestled in the corner of her room. She noticed a smiling young girl, which gave her stomach a nice sensation. This was her true happiness, but her grin gradually faded as she recalled her parents' talk. She crawled into her bed and went off to sleep as the tears streamed down her cheeks and onto her pillow.

billy felt the same way the next morning. It was the same as every other morning; she sprang out of bed, cleaned her teeth, put on her clothes, and dashed out the door. As was customary, she kissed her parents farewell, snatched the keys from the marble counter, flung her bag over her shoulder, and closed the door behind her. She strolled down the sidewalk and realised something was wrong as she passed her adversaries. They made no attempt to annoy her today. Perhaps God had heard her pleas. Perhaps she was imperceptible. She grinned to herself as she moved rapidly through the dense throng.

As she got closer to the school, the sky opened up and a gentle rain started to fall. She made her way up the steps and inside the school. Her damp footwear produced a tiny squeaking sound when they made contact with the cobblestone stairs. She stepped through the red and white door frame and entered quickly. Billy felt as if she were in a jar of marbles being rattled from every aspect as she proceeded down the corridors. Individuals are shoved into lockers and ridiculed for their peculiarities. This made her physically ill. When she eventually arrived in the classroom, she sat fast, recognising she had been a few minutes late.

Billy started doodling on her desk while the instructor took attendance.

"Billy James?" the instructor inquired.

"I'm here," she responded.

"I suppose she isn't here today," the instructor said gently as he marked her absent. billy started to have a strong discomfort in her bottom left chest area.

"I'm here," she said. Then it struck her. Nobody was able to see her. She was really imperceptible. Despite her assumption that this would be the happiest news of her life, she became quite frightened. She was at a loss for what to do. After a few moments of internal debate, she decided to walk up and touch the instructor on the shoulder.

"Who threw that?" he inquired, perplexed.

A kid at the front of the classroom asked, "Threw what?"

billy became a bright crimson colour pretty fast. She was speechless. Then she heard a faint flutter of giggles that grew into a torrent of laughing. Suddenly, a pencil was hurled at her by one of her classmates, whom she did not really like. She had the sensation of being confined in a chamber with no way out. All of this was a dream, a delusion. She longed once again that she might be invisible.

CHAPTER FIVE

First kiss

Everybody has a memory of their first kiss. Occasionally, it's with a first crush or a random child under the slide. Mine was with my closest pal from childhood. Maria Clark was her given name. She had brown hair that her mother elaborately braided and usually wore faded red overalls. We accomplished everything in unison. At times, we even performed things that we knew would land us in hot water. We discovered a DVD stuffed behind the TV stand one day, as if someone kicked it there while cleaning. Although it was clearly intended for adults, my mother was in the grocery store. We inserted it into the DVD player and hit play. I can't recall the title, but halfway through, we saw something we had never seen before - two females kissing. Neither of us had ever witnessed a female kiss another girl; we had no idea it was even permitted. We agreed that since we were best friends, we should as well. We kissed while seated on an old brown fading couch in my living room.

Nobody recalls precisely how their first kiss feels, and definitely not me, but you remember how it feels - it felt right. We made a pledge to her mother before she was picked up that we would never tell anybody about the movie or the kiss. As Ms. Clark's blue station waggon approached, I stood on my creaking, wooden porch and waved farewell to her. Before she entered, she raced back and offered me a friendship bracelet. Pink and orange yarn were used to braid it. She secured it around my wrist and compelled me to swear I would never remove it.

The next day, Maria did not report to school. When I inquired as to the whereabouts of Maria, Ms. Wilson said that she was unaware of such a person. I thought it was strange, but Ms. Wilson was elderly and had an excessive number of pupils; maybe she forgot since she wasn't there that day. As soon as I stepped off the bus, I hurried inside and begged my mother if I might visit Maria's house after I did my schoolwork. She inquired as to who Maria was. I chuckled and informed her that she was being amusing herself. She made an odd look that I couldn't decipher. I hadn't seen it much at the time, but I've since watched it more times than I can count. I've since learned that it was a look of worry.

Days passed and Maria failed to report to school. I continued inquiring about her, and she insisted that I did not have a buddy called Maria. I attempted to show her the bracelet that Maria had fashioned for me, which remained securely fastened to my wrist as promised. She informed me that I created that at school. After a week, I became enraged and went in search of Maria on my own. After school, I headed to her home. She lived only a few blocks away, and I'd gone there so often that I felt certain I could get there on my own. I arrived and knocked on her door. The only closed door was the screen door, which produced a metallic tinging sound when I pressed my hand against it. Maria's mother approached the door, her hair in rollers and a cigarette in her fingers. I was glad that she seemed to be in good health. "How are you?" she said. "Do you sell cookies or something?"

I chuckled. "Not at all, Mrs. Clark. I'm searching for Maria. She has been absent from school for many days. "Is she ill?"

She gave me a perplexed expression. "Are you certain you have the correct address? There is no Maria in this room."

"What are you referring to?" I inquired. "Maria is your daughter, and I consider her to be my closest friend. We attend the same school."

"Oh, now I know you," she remarked. "You're the Bailey girl." You're a year younger than my kid, Grant."

"Indeed, I am enrolled in the same class as Maria."

"I'm not familiar with a Maria," she said sternly this time. "I have just two sons. Andrew and Grant. I am without a daughter."

I was becoming enraged. Why was everyone denying the existence of my dearest friend? "You do!" I lashed out at her. "Maria is your daughter," she said. She constantly wears faded red overalls that are nearly pink in colour. Every day, you braid her hair. And she made me this bracelet," I demonstrated the jewellery by holding up my wrist. "How come everyone continues to tell me she does not exist?" I burst into tears. Why was it that I was the only one who recalled Maria?

Mrs. Clark eventually called my mother and she escorted me home. I skipped school the next day and the day after that. When I returned, there was still no sign of Maria and no one who believed me. My mother then enrolled me in treatment. Dr. Treeman informed my mother that I have an overactive imagination and had developed an imaginary companion who seemed to be real. I knew Maria wasn't a figment of my imagination. After years of counselling and being taught Maria was not real, I discovered it was better to pretend she never existed. Years passed. After graduating from high school, I enrolled in a tiny liberal arts institution to pursue a degree in linguistics. Although the bracelet had long ago disintegrated, I kept it in a jewellery box on my vanity.

I hadn't kissed anybody since and had no intention of doing so. That is, until I met Renee Beaton in my sophomore year. Em was stunning. She was tall and had dark complexion, with braided hair that she usually wore in a bun. Her earrings were gold, and a matching gold ring dangled from her nose. She was always a more daring dresser than I, not hesitant to experiment with vibrant colours and patterns. She studied in digital media art, and her work demonstrates why. She once painted a girl with butterfly hair for me. Golden droplets cascaded down the canvas, prompting some of the butterflies to flee as though fleeing. It hung just below my bed in my bedroom, the ideal location for it to be the first thing I saw in the morning and the last thing I saw at night.

She instilled in me a newfound appreciation for art and introduced me to K-pop. As a white girl from the Midwest, I was unaware of K-pop. Whenever we had study sessions, she would track out some band I'd never heard of and we'd jam. On weekends, we'd visit art galleries and she'd educate me about the many painters we saw. We often went out together, but today was different since I intended to convey my emotions. It had been so long since Maria had vanished, and how could I be certain I was the one who did it?

We headed to our neighborhood's favourite tavern. It wasn't a college student hangout, so it was rather quiet, but the floor was sticky with booze and the air smelled strongly of beer. There were old torn-up pool tables in the corner, with two pool sticks waiting to be shattered in a drunken bar brawl, and a few lights were usually out, making the pub seem much dirtier and more dreary than it actually was. Em donned black and white lightning bolt leggings and a bright yellow leather jacket. Golden hoops adorned her locks, amplifying the impact of her jewels.

We spent hours drinking and conversing. She informed me of a large portfolio she needed to complete, and I informed her of a collaborative project I was essentially working alone. We discussed our hometowns, families, and which BTS member was our favourite. She quickly ensnared me in game after round of pool. I was attempting to focus, but I couldn't take my gaze away from her. My anxieties caused my hands to become so perspiring that I could hardly grasp the pool stick without it sliding through my fingers. We eventually returned and she escorted me to my dorm. She was saying her last farewells, and I realised this was it. I'd fumbled it. I didn't express my feelings to her, and I wasn't sure I'd ever find the guts to. She leaned in and kissed me just as I was about to give up hope. I recall precisely how this one felt. Her lips were soft and warm to the touch. She clutched me tight and I followed suit. My heart was burning with desire - I wanted more. Following that, I invited her upstairs, and it was at moments like these that I was delighted I lived in a single. We stayed up all night together. Everything was beginning to come together. I would finally be content, and Maria would leave me alone.

I awoke the following morning to find her gone. Assuming she had an early lesson, I didn't fret. I went to my Psychology lesson as usual and decided to see her later. I knocked on her door and was greeted by her roommate. She informed me that no one called Renee resided in this house. I was certain this was Em's dorm, although she may have been avoiding me. Perhaps she regretted it and instructed her roommate to remove me. I began to panic. Knowing she worked every Friday afternoon at the university coffee shop, I rushed over there. When I approached the desk, Kevin (a mutual buddy) was at the register. I inquired as to whether Em was employed, and he inquired as to who Em was. When I urged him to quit fiddling, he gave me a really perplexed face.

"You know about yea height, braided hair, nose ring," I replied, holding out my hand. He just shrugged and inquired as to my well-being. I remained silent and rushed out. How is it possible that this might happen again?

I walked into my room and logged onto my laptop. On Instagram, I looked for her account ArtWithEm32. Then there's Twitter. I even checked Facebook and discovered that all of her accounts had been deleted. I checked my contacts and couldn't find her number. I went to my gallery and saw that all of our photographs were vanished. I screamed and dashed to my wall. We had shot at least 10 polaroid images together. You couldn't erase such a piece of concrete proof, correct? I removed them one by one from my wall. She was not present at any of them. Even the one from New Years that featured just her was simply a snapshot of a chair with no one in it. I turned and saw the picture she had created for me was still hanging there, looking just as it had the day she presented it to me. I searched through my jewellery box and discovered that my friendship bracelet was still in its original location. I threw open my door when I heard a knock, thinking it was her.

“Woah.” Kevin was the culprit. "I've come to see how you're doing." According to his face, I seemed to be in a state of disarray.

"How did I get this?" I inquired, indicating the artwork.

"Is that the painting?" He enquired. I gave a nod. "I believe you acquired it on our thrifting excursion in Portland."

"No," I almost screamed, "Em did this for me." You recall? Em? Our ally?" His face shifted into the worried expression my mother gave me, which caused me to flush. I ejected him, my senses flooded with rage.

Following that day, I attempted to locate someone who remembered her. I inquired of the bartender at a pub we frequented and the librarian who always shouted at us for being too loud in the library. Nobody recalled her. I soon quit attending lessons. Then I ceased to leave my room. My raging rage had transformed into a sea of melancholy, and I was sinking. My mother persuaded me to take a leave of absence in order to cleanse my mind. She believed that all the liberal art jargon was getting to me. I was unable to inform her about Em. She would have committed me if she believed I was fabricating people once again. I returned to Dr. Treeman without informing her. I didn't even inform him of my true presence.

Years passed and I never returned to school. I left and found work as a bartender. It was a far cry from the run-down dive bar Em and I frequented. It was a posh nightclub that held several VIP events. It was constantly crowded, but the patrons left generous tips. After college, I didn't date. My buddies urged me to go out, but I couldn't take the chance. Even if no one believed me, I knew Maria and Em were actual individuals who would vanish regardless of what I did. Whenever I considered their whereabouts, I hoped they were safe and happy. I considered terminating everything all at once, just to be certain I didn't do this to anybody else. I suddenly understood that if I was gone, they were also gone. Nobody would remember them. I placed

Em's picture on the wall in my room with Maria's bracelet to ensure I would never forget them.

I was finishing up with my colleague Beth one night. Beth Josh worked as a bartender at the club as well. She was 25 years old and had just relocated to town. Her jet black hair was chopped short, and her makeup was always dark and gaudy. She was a diligent worker who got along with everyone. She's only been working at the club for six months, but during that time, we've come a long way. On evenings when we worked together, we would have a drink before calling it a night. It was great having the whole pub to ourselves. We drank more than usual that night and switched on the LEDs that bordered the main bar. The lights splashed rainbows over the room. Beth blared hip-hop music from her phone, and we all piled into the bar and danced. It was fantastic to let loose and have some fun. I was forced to pause after a few songs. We both crashed against the bar's side. She rested her head on my shoulder and sipped from her drink once more.

"You know," she began, her voice slurred, "I truly like you."

"I like you too," I chuckled as I glanced down at her. Additionally, my sentences came out in a slur, which made me laugh even harder. I was unaware of what was occurring throughout my laugh fit. Beth brushed her lips against mine as she moved forward. I pushed her with all my might, but it was too late. We exchanged kisses. I sprang off the bar, my body trembling with panic. She sincerely apologised. I was unable to look at her. She halted her music and approached me.

"I'm very sorry," she said. "I was under the impression that we were on the same page. "I —." I dashed out of the pub before she could continue. I entered my vehicle and dropped the keys while attempting to insert them into the ignition. I flew out of there and made a hasty return home. I entered my driveway and unlocked my phone. I began poring through my photographs, seeking images of Beth in an attempt to recall her face. Her elf-like nose and her sweeping black bangs. Her face was freckled and her eyes were hazel. I gazed at the photographs for as long as I could until tears blurred my vision and I lost sight of her.

I entered and took a position in front of Renee's picture. My palm was placed against the raised golden paint droplets. I studied the vibrant butterflies that seemed to fly off the page. My focus turned to the bracelet. Due to age, the orange had faded to a shade of brown, while the pink had become paler and sun-bleached. I lacked Beth's possessions. I wasn't sure how I was going to recall her. I turned out my light and sat on my bed, peering into the void. As with Renee and Maria, I would be the only recollector of her. There will be no Beth Josh tomorrow.

Printed by Libri Plureos GmbH in Hamburg,
Germany